A FAMOUS BROKEN HEART

A FAMOUS BROKEN HEART

A FANTASY NOVEL

Ann Druyan

University of Minnesota Press
Minneapolis
London

Published by the University of Minnesota Press
111 Third Avenue South, Suite 290
Minneapolis, MN 55401-2520
http://www.upress.umn.edu

ISBN 978-1-5179-2082-1 (pb)

A Cataloging-in-Publication record for this book is available
from the Library of Congress.

Printed in the United States of America on acid-free paper

34 33 32 31 30 29 28 27 26 25 10 9 8 7 6 5 4 3 2 1

FOR MY
MOTHER & FATHER

GOD CREATED HUMAN BEINGS
BECAUSE HE LOVED STORIES.

—RABBI ISRAEL OF RISHIN

CONTENTS

A FAMOUS BROKEN HEART

I

BENDING ASIDE & FALLING AWAY

SOMETHING BIG MUST HAVE happened in the night because there she was, waking up in yesterday's chalky clothes on a park bench with nothing between her and the sun, in a place too clean and casually botanical to be Queens.

A handsome man in a hot caramel gabardine suit was standing nearby and inquiring in cheerful way whether she might be Shakespeare.

"Well, is Shakespeare the name or no?" he asked like some helpful orderly coaching an inexperienced lunatic.

Marina opened her eyes for a moment, but the light was too bright for keeping them open. She shut them tight and tried to sneak back into her dream.

"Excuse me," he said, his face was so near that through her sleep's unfocused logic she supposed he was either a dog or deer. "Excuse me, but can you tell me if you are any writer at all?"

Marina didn't move or answer. She was still hoping to be re-instated to her dream, a stunning vision of twin constellations, wide-open v's on their sides, described by seven big diamonds each. Her psyche's astronomers had identified them as "the Chevrons." She clenched her eyes in an attempt to squeeze out any incriminating light. She just wanted one more look at the Chevrons crossing the spring night sky at the graceful, steady, airless pace of outer space.

But the man continued to hover over her, a cold, arousing shadow, so she gave in and woke up.

His sweet face was the first thing that she saw. It looked about thirty-five and apart from a few sexy dents almost new. The eyes were brown and round like her own, but the hair was fair and curly.

"Unpublished, perhaps?" he suggested eagerly.

Marina rubbed her eyes until she saw flash bulb patterns rising high like flying saucers, smoothly on a steady diagonal. She rubbed her eyes, until they squeaked in their sockets like wet shoes. It changed nothing. She was still in the wrong place. And the dapper stranger was right there, too, his friendly mouth poised for an answer.

Marina felt desperate for something familiar. She looked down at herself. It was reassuring to see her beloved white tee shirt with the red shooting gallery rows of baby ducks, the baggy jeans and the yellow sneakers trimmed in blue like houses in Connecticut. If it was true that you could be yanked out of your real life without any warning, and if in fact this was the case with her, at least she was wearing her most comfortable clothes.

The tinkly gold bracelet dangling on her right wrist was another consolation. Her father had given it to her in an unforgettable secret gesture when she was a little girl. She never outgrew it. Good diet and experimental medicines at that same tender age had stretched her long and lean in the vogue of local time.

"No," she yawned and shook her head. "Not Shakespeare."

"I'm not really surprised," he confided. "But you understand why I felt I had to ask. When it comes to Shakespeare, I don't know anything. And human sexual organization being the botch that it is, gender never stops me from asking questions.

"So," he said, "it was just a long shot. We . . ." His voice trailed off and he retreated two steps. He lowered his eyes as she was lifting hers.

There was nothing positively bizarre about the park—no blue animals, no rubies lying around to confirm that she was still within the jurisdiction of a dream. However, Marina sensed in some chilly, non-specific way that this semblance of reality was subtly imperfect like a "What is wrong with this picture?" puzzle.

She braced herself for the horrible slow-dawning discrepancy.

"Please don't let it be a noseless face in the trees," she prayed before she felt up to scanning the park.

The man's suit and the morning's dry cool air suggested a temperate latitude, but the plants seemed to grow with tropical confidence. They were members of the serious variety that can't be bothered with flowers. The fat arteries of their velvety leaves indicated lavish internal traffic; caravans of molecules on the move, trading heavy green secrets for light and rain.

Marina studied the stranger. He had two hands of five fingers and everthing else seemed in order. Oh, maybe the sun was hanging one upsetting inch too close. It could've been worse. She'd been spared the moving eyes in the painting. "I've eaten meat and I've yelled at my mother," she thought. "I've killed country bugs. I've rushed past the blind. Now a hungry person has hit me over the head and I'm dead and it's not fair."

The stranger sat down beside her, slapped her on the back and gushed, "It's Herman Melville, isn't it? Herman, Herman, how long we've been waiting for you! There's someone here I think you'll be glad to see," he teased with a sticky pleasure unbecoming to his height. "Now we'll just rush right over to the ceremony and you can enchant us with all you know about the mysteries of the South Seas and the quirky practices you couldn't write about back then and Nature's unknowable genius and the wildness of . . . "

"Please stop it. You're making me nervous. I'm not a famous writer. I'm lost and you're scaring me."

It wasn't like Marina to be direct with strangers. She was so timid in her heart's voice that sometimes the words wouldn't come at all to order from a waitress or to state her business to anyone. Her number had been called in bakeries and often she left without ever expressing her desires. In spite of this and her shaky hands, she was for personal reasons a hero to herself.

"I guess I knew you weren't Herman all along," he admitted. "George Eliot?" It was just a flicker of a question.

"No!"

"You wouldn't happen to be any relation to . . ."

"No, I wouldn't!" she snapped. "Listen. I want you to quit asking me if I'm famous writers. My name is Marina and I want to know where I am!"

"Marina who?" he asked.

Noticing her hesitation he volunteered, "Like Sophocles and Sappho? No last name? Just Marina?" He took a light hold of her hand. "A very great pleasure. Really."

His openness made her feel ashamed. "No, I've got a last name but it's terrible. It's so awful I'd rather not say."

She looked sullen. It made him unhappy. "Even the most loving authors can be unintentionally cruel," he observed. "They just don't foresee the everday life consequences. They forget that we have to write checks.

"But a name is something we make. If you had been Mr. Shakespeare," he twitted softly, "you would have known that. My own name is Armando Pigowitz," he lied. "It's not exactly music, but in this town I think it stands for something."

He was preachy but gentle, and apart from his wacko fixation with literature, he seemed like a regular guy.

"Mr. Pigowitz . . ."

"Armando, please, for reasons that are surely obvious."

"Alright, Armando. Where are we? I live in New

York City. Last night I was on my way to Queens to visit my parents. The last thing I clearly remember was riding down choppy Queens Boulevard in a big yellow Checker. That's the last thing."

This magnificent place is In The Beginning," he said as if that would clear it all up.

"In the beginning of what, Armando?" she asked patiently.

"Of everything, of course." He searched her eyes in vain for the recognition he expected.

"Oh boy." She took a deep breath. She gripped the smooth wood of the park bench with both hands. "Am I dead, Armando?" she asked solemnly. "Am I the size of a fork?"

"What an idea, Marina!" He laughed to himself. "No, you're alive and forks are much smaller than you."

"You know I'm no kid," she told him in her "I-pay-taxes" tone of voice. "I'm twenty-four. That's way too smart for the and-then-I-woke-up. That's just too old for the wonderland business."

She was getting fidgety and he wanted to help. He decided to try a little something he'd picked up from Tom Sawyer.

"I'm sorry I don't know about Queens. But nobody has ever complained before of being in this splendid community of fresh starts. I can assure you most are simply enchanted.' He dabbed at a non-existent tear with a silk handkerchief.

"Okay, Armando. No offense. I meant no harm. This

looks like a great place. Only I've already started elsewhere. I'd just like to go back."

He kept his head down.

"Or at least phone," she said, hoping to mollify. "Otherwise, my parents will call the police. They may have done this already."

He looked away.

"I just hope this isn't going to be one of those places where it's always sunny and everybody's white and chickens talk. I really couldn't stand that."

"No." It was a tiny, pathetic, high-pitched syllable which in no way devalued the deed to his sulk.

"Aw, come on, Armando," she pleaded. "I'm sorry if I hurt your feelings. I didn't mean to. I must be a little shocky. Forgive me. Come on," she coaxed, "tell me about this wonderful place."

He came to life abruptly, filling out like a paper fish dropped in a glass of water.

"How would you describe Paradise?" he asked her. "What would you say about Eden before God became disillusioned? About the whole wide world before people believed in belongings?

"My new friend," he said, putting his arm around her, "your awakening this morning was exactly that! And so much more than merely getting out of bed. You're in In The Beginning, a borough of dawns, where honest intentions are the order of each newly seen day. A fair land of first lines where ideas arise and rub their eyes and spring upon the unsuspecting. In short, the land of promises."

"Oh, brother." Marina staggered away from the park bench. "I'm just at the age when time speeds up in an odd way," she said. "Do you know what I mean? The winters come closer together and you begin to accept that you're not special anymore. And then," she said without pointing to any specific feature, but rather in a broad nod of impartial deference for the whole unlikely landscape, this.

"Why don't you come with me?" he asked. "I'm going to the celebration in town. Maybe someone there will have news of your Queens. If I may say so, you don't seem to have anything better to do and I know you'll find it diverting."

"What's the party for?" she asked half-heartedly.

"Is nothing taught in Queens?" he sniffed. "It's the Glorious Fuss, a ceremony unmatched in all the world's worlds for its beauty."

They walked without talking towards a walled town. Its rooftops made a modest low scallop against the sky.

"It might be Europe," she thought.

Over the town gate hung a banner with proud red letters proclaiming, "EVERYTHING GREAT STARTS HERE!" They paused beneath it to allow an acquaintance of Armando's to catch up with them. The man in the distance ran a few yards towards them, then walked, shrugging his shoulders and laughing, then ran again.

Marina's thoughts were stuck in an emergency loop. "I have to get in touch with my parents. They must be frantic. I better call them. I can't. There isn't any way. I don't think I'm in the world anymore . . ."

The man was with them now. He was another curly-headed guy, shorter and stronger than Armando, with stirred-up blue eyes. His skin was a well-tanned honey shade, not young but hardly wrinkled.

"This is Marina," Armando said. "I just met her this morning."

Taking her two small hands in his large knotty one, the man grinned. It was the smile of a person who loved to be scared.

"They call me Ishmael," he said.

"That's okay," she told herself. "Most of me must still be fast asleep."

II
EVERY READER'S RED

TOO BEAUTIFUL TO HAVE ever actually been seen, In The Beginning looked just the way you would remember it. There was every color in that town and in each one there was a milkiness to make it more like a memory.

There were statues. No generals on horseback, no statesmen. Just the characters of books and stories and poems, fashioned out of pressed birdseed, attracting an astounding variety of flying creatures. Daily the birds came, nibbling Nose of Cyrano for an ample main course and perhaps hunchback of Richard for dessert, making frequent passes at the numerous fountains for their beverage.

The citizens took great pleasure in the glory of the bird's feathers and the grace of their flight and were vigilant in replenishing the pedestals of the town with delicious villains and nourishing heroes and the equally tasty characters who fall somewhere in between.

The architecture was tempestuous in the spirit of movies. Facades dipped and arched with the details of wedding cakes. Some of the interiors were vast like the mythy continental ski lodges of thirties musicals. Some were simple and small like the homes of poor pretty girls.

It was clean. The streets were airy and wide, filled with all kinds of people, rushing towards Genesis Square in the center.

They looked miserable.

Armando spoke before Marina could ask why.

"You've been to New York, haven't you Ishmael?"

"Oh yes, I've been there." A fleet of sailor's recollections rowed across his face, giving them both the impression that only half of him remained there with them.

The other half boarded a freighter bound for New York, disembarked after an uneventful journey, ordered an ale at a Fulton Street tavern and planned a big night in Manhattan. By nine that same evening he was already in trouble with the authorities and anxious to rejoin the conversation.

"New York is my favorite city," he said, "and we all know I've seen quite a few. The languages and foods—and it's so busy! The way the buildings come up so quick like a constant storm around the harbor! I'd give anything," he said, pausing to savor some unexpressed fantasy, "anything at all to be written there. Is that where you're from, Marina?"

"Yes. But what do you mean, 'written there'?"

She was noticing that the serious residents of In The Beginning weren't simply depressed. They were nervous, too. They had the odd habit of looking up at the sky every other moment as if they expected something to fall.

Marina supposed it must have something to do with the birds.

"Written there. You know, someone, somewhere, sits down with a pen or a typewriter and they think up a body for you and a history and an accent and a way of looking at the world and the next thing you know, you're shopping in Persia or hanging around Paris or, if you're not lucky, getting your teeth fixed in Peru. There's never any telling.

"Sometimes you get mighty angry because you've made other plans and there isn't even enough time to get someone in to water the plants. But there's something much worse than the bother and the unforeseen peril and that's not to be written at all."

As soon as Ishmael said this he realized that he'd done a terrible thing.

Armando just shrugged his shoulders. His chin almost to the middle button of his shirt, he made an empty 'that's alright' gesture.

"Roger, I'm so stupid. You know I'd never deliberately say or do anything to injure you."

"Roger? I thought you said your name was Armando."

"His name is Roger Frommage," Ishmael interjected.

"Armando, Roger . . . It could be Sadie for all I care. You see, it doesn't make one bit of difference to me. I've never been written and if things go on like this I don't think I'll care much longer. It's just not worth it." He stopped talking for a moment because he was afraid he would cry.

"It's not that I'm complaining," he grumbled. "I remember the day I saw Romeo off. We were having lunch at the cafe by the square on a splendid sunny afternoon when he got the call. 'You'll be next, Roger,' he told me. 'I just know it,' he said and was gone to glory and I was left sitting there, stuck with two fettucines and the check.

"Do I have to tell you how long ago that was?" Marina and Ishmael shook their heads. "But did I lose faith? Did I crumble? NO!

"I kept on struggling with the bitterness that grew within me. I tried to be happy for my more fortunate friends."

Roger made a show of hopping a few feet away.

"Oh, really, Don Quijote?" he said, impugning the vacant air. "You don't say? It sounds divine. And you say Sancho Panza and Dulcinea will be going along with you? How marvelous. Be sure to give them my best," he called to the invisible Spaniard.

"Years passed. Centuries passed! 'Bon Voyage, Sidney Carton. Sayonara, Genjisan. Dress warm, Emma Bovary. So long, Gunga Din.'

"Oh, but it was the March sisters that really drove me up the wall. When the four syrupy sisters left all at once I must confess I considered the window."

He turned abruptly to stare down a listening bystander in a satin bowling jacket. Roger was too upset to be disconcerted.

"That's why I take these long walks. Always hoping that maybe this day I'll run into a writer. But it's all very futile. Writers never come here . . . except when they've been written, of course.

"You tell yourself things like 'Relax, your time will come. They're probably saving you for an epic.' Well I don't mind telling you that at this point I'd take a walk-on in a trash novel. Anything. Any written thing at all."

His voice breaking, he collapsed. Arms tight around knees up against his chest, he shook and he sobbed. Ishmael's heart twisted up with longing to relieve his sorrow.

Marina didn't know how to react. For seconds at a time she felt sorry for the guy, but each time she remembered what his problem was it made her feel like an idiot.

"I wish you the best of luck," she told the stooped and quaking figure," but, I've really got to get out of here."

"Then, by all means, get going," Ishmael shouted. He couldn't fathom cruelty.

"I'm not a hard person," Marina insisted. "I hope he gets written." Ishmael was unconvinced. He sank down next to Roger and put his arm around him.

"Roger, look at it this way," Marina implored. "Once you're written, that's it, right? You get to have an adventure but after that it's downhill all the way, isn't it? You're a has-been for ever after."

"No, no. You don't understand at all." Roger gulped. His nose was stuffing up. Marina and Ishmael could hardly make out what he was saying.

"It's not that way. Every time someone reads you, you get to go again . . . Ishmael gets to go all the time!" It was more than he could bear to contemplate. A fresh spate of tears rushed out of Roger and he resumed his despondent moaning and rocking.

"You mean over and over. That doesn't sound so great. I'd hate it. The same battles and the same weddings year after year?" Marina knelt close to Roger and whispered in his ear. "You seem much too interesting for that kind of life. Much too grand."

Roger didn't respond. If anything, he appeared even more despondent.

Ishmael touched Marina's shoulder and beckoned her to move with him a few feet away from their desolate comrade. Once they were out of earshot he began to explain.

"It's always wonderfully different, Marina. A book isn't like anything else at all. We tell our secrets silently to one person at a time and it always comes out a little changed. You must know how it is from your own experience. When you come back from your trip to Europe you'll tell some people about the palaces and food and others about the men.

"You could read me now and together we'd take one kind of voyage. But read me again in fifteen years, when you've had some time to lose a couple of things that you love and to love things you can't possibly imagine today. Let me promise you, Marina, it will be a journey of quite another sort that we will make then.

"And, as unalike as those will be, another persons's would be still more remote. In fact, it would be downright unrecognizable."

Marina was skeptical.

"But why? It's always the same story, the same descriptions, the same outcome. You always have the same lines to say. They don't change. They can't. It's a printed thing; the same for me to see as it would be for anyone, now and years from now."

"Yes. Exactly. But what do you see it with?"

Marina didn't know what he was after.

"You see it with that most vital and human of organs, the mind's eye. That's an unlimited field of vision. Not a hedge or horizon that can stop it.

"Think of it, Marina! No license. No budget. Readers are like snowflakes and fingerprints," he rhapsodized. "Distinction is their commonality.

"Once you've been written the possibilities are infinite. Each with a perfectly unique set of memories and a vision, therefore, unprecedented. Every reader's red is really another color."

"But what happens if your book gets picked up by a real fool? You know, someone who has no imagination at all?"

"I can't deny that some times are better than others." From the expression on Ishmael's face, Marina knew that he was remembering some especially sluggish jaunts on the Pequod. "Sure, you get your share of the dullards. But, believe me, darling, a good book is hard to stop."

The two became quiet. All that was left of Roger's lament was a low sigh. It pierced them both.

"Roger will be written," Marina heard herself declare. And Roger heard her, also. But, he was too exhausted to reply.

"Yes, honey," he said in his heart, "you do it. You write me down. I'll wait. What's a little longer? I'll be patient. As patient, honey, as words on a page."

III
ROMAN CEMENT

THEY WERE ALL THE WAY to Genesis Square without saying a word.

Marina was running through an important old memory. Her parents took her on a driving trip when she was a child. She sat in the back seat feeling small. They passed hundreds of billboards and she tried not to read every one. Marina hoped they would round a bend and there up ahead would be an ad or a warning that she couldn't read.

But even so long ago it was already too late. She could read, and so far this was just making the world smaller. Before, the signs might be saying anything. The pictures were lovely. But comprehension became involuntary. Once she got the message she knew that most of them were merely instructions and more of them were lies. She read the signs. Accepting what was dealt to her, she took the words and ripped them apart, reorganizing them on behalf of a need she couldn't have named at the time. A "speed limit" was shattered and reassembled into the phrase "time lisped." ("Souvenirs" were "sour vines," and "Cheap cars" became a "space arch" or a "peach scar.") "Now I'll take the words and make a person," she thought. "I'll make a person the way that they have made a world."

The afternoon sun dazzled off the sheen of the costumes and banners of the Fuss. The sharp light made her sneeze. The gloomy populace shifted from foot to foot between the band shell festooned with tiger lilies at the southern end and the similarly bedecked speaker's platform at the northern end. A thousand multi-colored silk triangles slapped at a thousand white poles in the wind. Everything was waiting.

Roger was preoccupied trying to pump some conviction into a faint hope. He didn't notice Ishmael's arm snaking through his for guidance and support.

"It's true she's young and not a professional," he told himself. "But . . . suppose I was a melody. Yes, I was a tune like a butterfly floating from music room to music room trying to insinuate myself into the heart of a composer. Whispering myself again and again into the ears of unhearing musicians, only to be flicked away.

"Let's say I was the Symphony #1 in E flat major and after ages of being ignored an eight year old came along and announced, 'Tune, I'll write you down.' It would seem ridiculous . . . unless of course the little dear happened to be Mozart. And then it wouldn't be silly at all.

"She has to be the one. Oh please, please, couldn't she be the one?"

Ishmael was worried. He'd seen small boats set out on wild oceans before. He knew Marina meant well. (But what if writing Roger was simply beyond her?) Roger's spirit was too rare to toy with.

"Marina, I've got to talk with you. I must know how you intend to accomplish this. It's very nice that you want to help our friend, but, take my word, there's more to this writing business than you think." His voice was stiff with apprehension.

"First tell me, would it have to be published in order to do Roger any good?" She was unafraid.

"Not necessary," Roger piped in. "Why, some of my best friends are unpublished. See that tall woman in the yellow mackintosh, standing over there by the speaker's platform? She's right there, talking to the butcher. That's Veronique Butts, a remarkable person. Kidnapped by a homely man from her apartment on the upper west side of your own city. He was absolutely mad about her and didn't know what else to do. Took her to North Africa on some revolutionary pretext.

"She happened in a first novel by a fireman. So far she's only been read by a couple of relatives and a friend of a friend whose brother-in-law is supposed to have connections. But who knows, right?

"At least she can tell you what she's about."

The Glorious Fuss was about to get underway. The crowd grew silent for a moment until the stillness was broken by the first strains of their anthem. The all-volunteer orchestra played passionately. The people sang with deep feeling. There was no looking around. They were rapt.

Citizens of the imagination,
Creatures of the mind and heart,
Honor this solemn obligation
Every character must play a part…

"Okay," Marina said. "This is the deal. If you guys can help me get back to Queens…"

"Ah Queens," Ishmael mused. "That sleepy pastureland at the feet of the Long Island, across the water from Manhattan. I know it well."

"I guess it's been a while, huh?" Marina rolled her eyes. "Get me back to Queens or any part of the Greater New York area and I'll write you myself. Not only will I write you, but, if I have to, I'll spend the rest of my life paying people to read you! I can't promise to make you a household word or anything. But you will be written."

May the readers hear our breathing,
May they feel our awful pain,
The world of human beings is seething
Pray, Our dreams will make them sane…

"Do you really think you can, Marina?" Roger's face was so near to hers that their noses touched. "Really?"

"I'm smart and I'll do my best," she told him.

"Oh, yes, Marina! Write me! Give me allergies and prejudices! A cause . . . A crime . . . A reason! Write me enemies to fantasize my downfall. And loved ones to be concerned if I'm ever late.

"Send me anywhere! To a dull job or a fatal disease. To the Sahara where I would be delighted to die of thirst. To a life of quiet desperation behind a desk in India! To an ill-fated government robbery attempt! Let me languish for the love of someone unworthy, anywhere!"

March across a million pages
Till it cannot be denied
That the wisdom of the ages
Will not be flaunted or defied . . .

Marina was trying to tell him to take it easy, but Roger's eyes were glazed with exotic possibilities.

"Frustrate me! Ruin my plans. You're the boss. Just write me, honey. That's all I ask. Write me down."

Know there is but one true glory
Let the rest be ash and dust.
All the world tells one great story
Now make it real with love and trust!

The song was ended and the crowd was hush. Even Roger was quiet. All that could be heard was the dry rustle of the very old lady's wedding dress as she mounted the platform.

IV

WHEN THE MUSIC CHANGES

BIRD SHADOWS FLECKED THE MOON as it sent its borrowed light through her gauzy veil and gauzy body. She was a flimsy, yellowed person with messy white hair; barely there for the eye to grab and hold, a broom in a bridal gown whose dried-up face and bony hands must be a mean trick, a chimaera of acute oppositions, half marrying, half crumbling, a preposterous sight, impossible, another piece of doddering reality.

"My fellow figments of the imagination," she began in a deep, strong voice that was confounding like her unshrunken eyes and all of her, "I am, as most of you know, Miss Havisham of *Great Expectations*—written, published, reprinted, translated and experienced countless times. I have out-lived my dear author, his copyright, our epoch. My heart is one of the more famous broken ones—never more grieved than tonight.

"This was to be our Glorious Fuss. It will not be. We cannot celebrate a way of life that at this very moment is made tense and joyless by a jeopardy most dreadful real." She paused for a moment while the enchanted crowd mumbled their cloudy consonance.

"All it ever was, was dreams. All we know is dreams.

For a golden age our world turned just right in the kindly blue thrall of imagination. It surrounded us and it enabled us to breathe. And we loved the place it came from.

"But something has gone terribly wrong there. Our sky grows shabby. Small holes of non-light appear above us. They are alarming and they make us cough. We may not go on living in this dream world. Such a darkening in our lives and we don't even know why.

"It was written that when the mode of the music changes, the walls of the city shake. They shake now. Could it be that a change in the music makes them tremble? Makes us all tremble?

"There were those, a while ago, who predicted that television would be our downfall. But I must say that I never took it very seriously. A lot of theft, illnesses and silly troubles, night after night. Could a thing so uneven threaten the likes of us?"

The crowd asked themselves that question. For a quiet sinking minute they searched for their nerve. Then a cyclops cupped his hands to his mouth and boomed, "NO!" over their heads. That spawned a chorus of "no's" which seemed to please Miss Havisham greatly.

"It *is* true that there has been an ominous increase in the number of mid-story abandonments. After a couple of pages you're back on the shelf, left perchance for the new and easy things that ask nothing in return?" The crowd became uneasy again. They didn't want to think about it.

"I've seen you," she said. "You wait till it's dark to dawdle down a side street; back early and ashamed. You tell your friends that the reader couldn't put you down. You call yourselves "gripping" and "insightful" or some other meaningless flattery picked up from those more recently written. You swear they had to finish your whole damn book in one night!"

Miss Havisham looked out across a sea of stooped shoulders and bowed heads. She tried to catch the eye of the sweet knucklehead cyclops, but even he was unwilling to be seen.

"The other world remains a mystery to us," she said in a kinder voice. "We know from their stories that they have a tendency to squander. Perhaps they've been improvident with their illusions. Maybe that's what causes our air to grow stale and our sky to grow thin.

"I don't know. But I can assure you that our survival depends upon our finding out. We must discover the cause and then we must find a way to reverse this horrendous process. Everything we treasure hangs in the balance."

The old bride had worked enough halls to know when she had them.

"I exhort you to join together and to try absolutely anything to avert this catastrophe. I implore you to be creative and audacious. Any conceivable solution, no matter how bizarre, must be explored. Look everywhere for our salvation."

"Yes, everywhere," someone cried out carried away.

"Perhaps we will fail. After all, what are we? Just nouns and verbs strung together for the sake of a memory or a notion. We're made by people notorious for spending too much time alone. Maybe we'll die here when it's all gray.

"If this is inevitable, take comfort. Be mindful of the power and beauty of endings. Remember that it's the last lines that make them swallow.

"If this is meant to be our own final chapter then let it come resonant with all the unruly glory of precious life.

"Our end must shake sufficiently to cause even that ragged heaven to shudder!" A sheath of rotten chantilly fell away from the stick fingers of her pointing right hand. "Let heaven turn upside down if something infinite can be abridged!"

V

A BAD BROWSE

EVERYBODY WAS BLUE except Ishmael.

Ishmael was red. Red and moving this way real fast and then that way real fast like a full-blown balloon released unsealed. High-pitched sea curses about hooks and knots escaped from the corners of his mouth. Marina was embarrassed and hoped the others wouldn't assume they were together.

"A fine time! Just a dandy time!" he hissed. And then as if it wouldn't be kept in another second, he succumbed to a fit of raucous, hysterical laughter.

"What's the matter with you?" Marina demanded.

He couldn't reply. He was laughing so hard he had to concentrate on breathing when he wasn't laughing.

"I really don't see what could be so funny on a sad night like this," she fumed. "Are you just plain nuts?"

"It's alright, Marina," Roger counseled. "Leave him alone. He'll be okay. It's just a particularly bad browse. It shouldn't last more than a couple of minutes."

"A bad browse?" She was fragile but she had a fine way of looking at people as if they were crazy.

"Forgive me." Roger was weary. "I keep forgetting that you're not one of us. It's hard to remember. I guess I feel as if I've always known you. I must say, I don't see any cause for resentment on your part."

"A bad browse?" she persisted.

"It usually happens when someone picks you up in a library or a shop. They flip through you to see if you're worth their time or not. It tickles. All that quick touching of little parts of your life can be quite a torment. I've heard that speed-readers often have the same terrible effect. Of course, that's something I wouldn't know first hand."

"Wait a minute. Let me get this straight. You're telling me that because someone happens to thumb through your book, you get like that?" Ishmael, in the deepest throes of his browse, was completely unaware of her angry, incredulous pointing.

"This is a dream, right?" Marina asked, hoped.

"I don't think so," Roger answered.

"How can you stand it?"

"I can't. Let's go home and get some sleep. I'm tired and tomorrow asks a lot of us all."

"But what about Ishmael? We can't just leave him here, howling and skipping around."

"Ishmael can take care of himself. He's a survivor. Besides, he's been through this many, many times before. It's part of his job, the lucky dog. Come on."

Roger lived in an ecru-colored stucco cottage with a ripply red Spanish tile roof. The front door opened directly into a homey living room. There was a fireplace, a vivid Persian rug and a simple wooden dinner table and four chairs. On the table there were lace place mats and an enormous lavender amaryllis in the center, trumpeting delicacy in four directions.

The walls were covered with informal portraits of friends endorsed with their extravagant affections. Gray, in a black and white photograph, playfully attempts to tousle Uriah Heap's matted hair. Uriah reaches up to stop him. Their free arms are around each other and they grin. "Dear Roger—Stick this picture in your closet. Who knows? It might get better. Love, Dorian and Stingy."

A photograph of a slender young woman in trousers standing on the struts of an old silk-winged plane bore the provocation. "Anytime—Hes," dashed off carelessly in cocoa brown ink. Another picture of a lady with a lamb had no inscription.

Porcelain figurines of young boys at static mischief stood on the mantelpiece and the glass shelves of a china closet by the door. Roger's bedroom and the kitchen were off to the left, through a short gallery. The guest room was to the right.

"It's funny. I've lived here forever and yet you, Marina, are my very first overnight guest." He presented her with fresh towels and a new cake of oatmeal soap. He kissed her on the forehead and wished her a good sleep.

It was a sweet little room with soft yellow walls and clean white molding. The curtains were the color of the moistest part of a honeydew melon. There was a chest of drawers, an easy chair and a small uncomplicated table by the bed. A charming painting of peas and watercress hung over the bed.

She was still sitting, running the day's wonder over and over in her head, when a few minutes later there was a gentle knock at the door.

"Come in."

Roger slowly elbowed the door open, both his arms round the mammoth amaryllis. He carefully placed it on the end table.

"Well, good night again. I'm glad it's you," he said so low that she almost didn't hear him.

VI

A COMMITTEE TO MEND HEAVEN

A MORNING BREEZE HELD the curtains at arm's length as Marina lay in bed, starving and staring at the ceiling. She didn't know what she was supposed to do. So she just stayed there, under the covers, waiting for Roger to make a sound.

After what seemed a very long time, the doorbell rang and a moment later there was a lot of sharp, happy noise coming from the kitchen. Marina jumped into her jeans and tee shirt, dashed out of her room and found Roger and Ishmael toasting each other with glasses of apricot juice.

"What happened? Is the sky going to be okay?"

"Marina, they picked me! Me, unwritten and unread!" Roger hopped a few feet away from where he'd been standing and struck a pose. "'I'm sorry, Sherlock, I'm afraid we have nothing for you today. It's Roger Frommage we'll be wanting for this job.'"

"That's terrific, Roger. What's the job?" Marina asked while pouring herself a glass of juice.

Roger didn't answer. Instead, he sat down at the table, leaned forward and pressing his index finger on the cover of a butter dish, he proceeded to affect a voice redolent with anger and authority.

"You say Rhett Butler and Miss Scarlet O'Hara are here to see me? Get rid of them. I don't care what you tell them. Have you gotten ahold of Frommage yet? WELL WHY NOT?"

"Roger, what's the job?"

"You mean to say that you expect me to settle for the Great Gatsby? Do you realize that there's still a chance that we might be able to get the Formidable Frommage? You must be kidding!"

"Roger . . ." Ishmael gave Marina a wink. Ishmael's whole face was a wink, crinkled up in appreciation for Roger's performance.

"Of course, there's no guarantee that Frommage will accept. He's a busy man. Just in case, better send somebody over to old Lear's place. Don't promise him anything. Just feel him out. Remember we only want Lear if we can't get Frommage."

"Get Frommage for what?" Marina shouted, laughing.

"For the committee," Roger answered in his own gentle voice. "The committee to save us all. They picked me to be on the committee."

"Roger, if I had a committee, you'd be the first person I'd want to have on it."

"Really? Do you really mean it? You don't think that I'm . . . silly?" Roger looked away from his own words.

"I do not. Listen, when your book does get written, and you can be sure it will, there's only one spot for you. Hero. 'Cause that's what you are. A natural star."

Roger toyed with the scalloped edge of the breakfast cloth and swallowed. Ishmael rose to busy up the silence.

"Our friend will be in mighty good company. Quite a bunch. Anna Karenina, Willy Loman, Uncle Tom, Athos, Moll Flanders and Miss Havisham, of course. La creme de la creme, so to speak. I can tell you that it's agreat comfort to me knowing the whole matter is in their very capable hands."

"When do you start?" Marina asked.

"This afternoon. Promptly at one o'clock in the banquet room of Il Paradiso, the best Italian restaurant in town. Northern Italian. It doesn't look like anything from the outside, but the food is divine. The scallopine is paper thin and the salads are crispy. I must take you there sometime, Marina."

Roger thought for a second and then, whirling around, he snapped his fingers. "I'll take you there today! That's right! To the meeting. You can be our first witness."

"Witness?"

"Exactly! You can testify before the committee. You, and, as far as I know, only you, can tell us what's gone wrong in the other world."

"I don't think so, Roger. I mean, I get nervous talking in front of people I don't know. My lips get cementy and I can't work my face right. I really don't want to."

"But Marina, am I to believe my ears? Afraid of Uncle

Tom? Of Madame Karenina? They're, all of them, lambs. Absolute fluff. And the Musketeer, why he's the biggest baa baa of them all. They'll love you. I promise."

"Roger, I'm sure they're great. It's not that. I just wouldn't be very good at it."

"It's not my place to tell you what to do," Ishmael said, slowly raising a mediating right hand. "But perhaps you don't fully realize how serious our situation has become. We are in trouble. This is the time to belay one's personal fears and pitch in. I beg you to reconsider. We depend on you."

Marina looked around the room. There was no getting out of it. After a moment, their eyes met and it was settled.

"Okay, okay. I'll do it. But I don't see how it will help anything."

"It will. It will." Roger clapped his hands and immediately began to consider what he would wear. Ishmael hugged her.

As they talked, Ramona Diamant, a student in Madison, Wisconsin, was washing her hair. After she brushed it, she made some instant soup and picked up a worn, coverless copy of *Moby Dick*. Ishmael looked like he'd been tapped on the shoulder and then he was gone.

Marina practiced intelligent facial expressions. Her mouth was dry and her throat needed constant clearing. From Roger's room she could hear his thin but heartfelt voice belting out an exultant rendition of "Our Love Is Here To Stay."

They say the Rockies may tumble,
Gibralter may crumble
They're only made of clay...

Then he was dressed, in the living room and ready to go. He looked marvelous in his white suit, accented elegantly by a foulard tie of diagonal pink and green stripes.

Il Paradiso was a five minute walk from Roger's home. He was right–it didn't look like anything from the outside. Just a flat, poured concrete building, distinguished only by its name, fashioned out of wrought iron, wriggling in an optimistic script above the entrance.

"I don't understand," Marina said."If this is such an important meeting, then why hold it here?"

"Do you know a better Italian restaurant in this town? While I admit the minestrone lately hasn't been what it once was, the baked clams..."

"No, no. I mean why don't you hold it in a city hall or a courthouse or some place official like that?"

Roger was perplexed. "We always hold our conferences at Il Paradiso."

Roger knew everyone in the restaurant. He stopped at each barstool and table, making friendly inquiries peppered with proper nouns. Then, with an outrageous air of self-possession, mumbling about having business elsewhere, he waltzed Marina through the door at the rear.

The banquet room of Il Paradiso was a very big place in a remarkably small space. The subterranean richness of the terra cotta color of the walls contrasted dramatically with the tormented gilt flourishes of thirty picture frames.

Within them were paintings of Greece and Italy, dark and uneventful like the ones English people were fond of in the nineteenth century. Shepherdesses plopped themselves down on broken pieces of the Parthenon, intent on sheep. Rascals reclined upon the Forum's weedy stumps. Their legs in the air, they teased themselves with wineskins held high above their faces. Every picture was a joke on glory.

A monumental chandelier hung from the ceiling. It looked as if a thousand giant countesses had decided to hang their earrings there. It was bad judgment on their part. There were no windows in the room, so the impeccably carved prisms has only the unsteady candlelight to transform.

All this in a room just large enough to comfortably surround one oval table for eight. The silverware was weighty, the crystal was light and the linens were sheets of Swiss snow.

Seated around this table was an elderly black man with an affable look, a middle-aged lady in an extremely low-cut blouse, a worn-out man in a shabby, gray business suit, an exquisite woman in a burgundy velvet dress trimmed with brown sable, Miss Havisham in her customary wedding gown, and a coarse-faced, mustachioed fellow wearing a hat with one stringy feather. He was the first to speak, glaring at Roger and menacing the air with a breadstick.

"Correct me if I'm mistaken, but I don't recall that the invitation mentioned anything about bringing a date." Some of the six seemed to find this remark amusing, but Roger was unruffled.

"A date, no. But a witness, perhaps."

"A witness?" Miss Havisham echoed dubiously.

"If I told them once I told them a thousand times," the weary man whispered to the beauty. "You can't trust these unwrittens. They're an unknown quantity. Too risky." She chose not to answer and pretended to consider a radish.

"Yes, a witness. It is my great pleasure to present to you Mademoiselle Marina, direct from the communications capital of the world in question." Hands on her shoulders, he moved the rigid Marina around as if she were a chair. "I've taken the liberty of engaging her assistance for the purposes of this forum. Marina," Roger said as he pointed each one out, "please meet Miss Havisham, Uncle Tom, Moll Flanders, Athos, Anna Karenina and Willy Loman."

"How did you get here?" Willy Loman demanded. "Were you written here? You'll have to go back. I'm sorry but you don't belong here. It's out of the question."

"I'd love to go back. Maybe you can tell me how," Marina snapped.

"Friends, fellow committee members, this is no time for squabbling," Roger appealed. "Don't you see, she's just what we need. A godsend. Marina can tell us things about the readers that we have no other way of knowing.

I confess I don't have any idea how she got here. But she is here."

"You can always tell a pro," Moll muttered to no one in particular, her crèpe décolletage rippling indignant. "The man has no experience. Trust Frommage to pull a wacky thing like this."

"But she is here," Roger repeated in exasperation. "And the question is, are we going to allow petty rivalries and wholesale grumpiness to shatter this opportunity to investigate conditions in her world? That being the very same world that we're so gravely concerned about." Roger picked up a napkin to fling down in disgust.

Miss Havisham called for and got order. She summoned a waiter named Vito and asked him to bring an extra chair and setting. Admonishing the group for their petulance, she insisted they order first. She disappeared behind a menu the size of a Monopoly board.

Uncle Tom counselled Marina to stay away from the minestrone. She took his advice and ordered the baked clams and sole franchese. Moll Flanders debated a long time about whether she should allow herself the sinful pleasure of a side order of pasta. She tried to persuade Anna Karenina to share it with her, but the Russian woman demurred.

"Go ahead and have it anyway, Birdbones," Athos called out with affectionate familiarity.

Moll smiled. "You're right. What the hell!" She slapped herself on the diaphragm. "The very same bodice

I wore on all me conquests. Done up and undone a thousand more times than any good girl would own up to. But not let out so much as a notch in all these years. Except when I was birthing. And you don't get that way from too much tortellini!" She jabbed Uncle Tom in the shoulder until he was forced to agree.

"Does Vito have a book?" Marina asked Miss Havisham while they waited for their food.

"What?" she said. "Our Vito? Why, don't tell me you've never heard of 'End the Beguine'?"

Marina was forced to admit she hadn't.

"No real reason you should have," the old bride confided. "It's a real dose of laudanum. A clinker. The story of two nice kids from the States who meet and fall in love against the sweeping panorama of Bogota during the early days of the Alianzo Para Progreso. Swill.

"Poor dear Vito got impressed into the role of the gross and stupid local chief of police. He's the one who's never properly buttoned. It's so unfair.

"Luckily, he rarely gets read. If ever there was a book meant to turn brown in the libraries of summer houses and failing cruise ships, 'End the Beguine' was it, my dear."

"That's too bad," Marina sighed. "At least he's only a minor character."

"No such creature, my young darling," Miss Havisham was quick to correct. "And Vito, here you are. We'd begun to wonder if you hadn't gone south."

After they were served, Miss Havisham tapped a teaspoon on a bread plate to get attention.

"I move that the first order of business should be to find out what this child can tell us. I trust there are no objections," she said, disregarding the pouting courtesan and the dour Musketeer. "Very well, speak, young lady. You have the floor."

Marina's whole life did not flash before her eyes. Just one outstanding incident. It was the time a platoon of summer campers went amok and painted her red. Because her parents were expected to visit the following day, the counselors worked through the night, tormenting her with cotton swabs dipped in nail polish remover. They took the paint off and a great deal of the young Marina, too. Later in life she had a strong feeling about a story in a Ripley's Believe-It-Or-Not book. It was about a man who was swallowed by a whale and emerged shortly after without any body hair at all. There was another man in that same volume who became transparent after spending eleven years sitting in olive oil. She continued to think about skin until something jolted her back to the difficulty of the moment.

From across the table Roger silently beseeched her to speak. She felt dusty, sallow and completely blank. Her toes curled in her sneakers like a parrot's.

Athos hmm-hmmed. He was aglow with "I told you so's." His pathetic plume gathered its last bit of stamina to gesture buoyant rebuke in her direction. Willy and Moll confirmed each other with pious nods. Miss Havisham looked surprised. Uncle Tom and Anna looked elsewhere. Roger looked sick.

And Roger was really beginning to matter.

"I'll tell you about the world," Marina said, trying her best to sound like a cop or a cowboy. "But I think I better warn you, it's not going to be pretty."

VII
MARX AND SPARKS

"IT'S NOT SIMPLE," she began. "The world is very small, tiny even, when you think about the universe. But big, as far as people are concerned. So big, that any time of the night or day you can imagine a person doing something. It could be anything. Mistreating an animal. Learning how to juggle. Planting beans. The world is big enough so that any of those things you could imagine are actually happening. That very minute.

"Even if it's very late at night. Someone's always awake in the world."

Fear left her. A slender woman can lift up a Buick if someone dear is trapped beneath. She was taken over by the same human magic that fueled and astonished our ancestors in their tense flights from the company of boars and tigers.

The committee relaxed into listening positions as Vito darted deftly among them, retrieving dinnerware.

"But of all those things you could think up for people to be doing, I think going hungry would have to be your safest bet. Going hungry, pushing each other around, leaving bombs, breaking promises, leaving nothing. It happens far away all the time. But sometimes near.

"We're almost two kinds of people. Some of us see it on the evening news or read about in the morning paper. And some of us get hurt.

"But, you know we all get hurt. Because even if you live in a very nice house like I do, sooner or later the lies and the fires have got to burn you. I know this for a fact."

"You mean to tell me," Uncle Tom demanded, the anger in his voice stealing space from the disbelief, nothing has changed in all this time?"

Anna Karenina placed her hand on his as if there was a fire right there that could be smothered.

"Don't be a child," Willy Loman barked. "Of course it's changed. Wasn't I there a hundred years after you? Wasn't I?"

Uncle Tom nodded. They all nodded.

"Sure I was and I'm telling you that you wouldn't have recognized the place," he declared, folding his arms.

"He's right," Marina granted, toneless and respectful. "In some ways it's changed."

"See? What'd I tell you?" There were sharp little chips of a laugh in Loman's voice. "Sure," he said haughtily as if he'd caught someone telling an old joke, "women vote, black people vote. No more plagues. They've got public schools and social security. They've got laws to protect everybody."

"But that's not all they got, Mr. Loman," Marina called out from some brave place in her city-made heart. "I have to tell you that every day of my adult life I've asked myself how people can stand it. Even lucky people. Because the truth is, Mr. Loman, personal happiness is at best a quick thing in a desperate world.

"That place you talk about, that's where I come from. And I was there even more recently than you. The last thing I remember was bumping up and down in the back seat of a big yellow cab. It was late at night and I could hardly read the newspaper I held in my hands. Had to keep waiting for the streetlights to glide over the page. It took a long time to read this one story about a new kind of bomb that kills people without damaging property. Boom! and for miles around people lie there, their eyes working like fish out of water. I tell you, Willy, those people back there are crazy."

Roger was watching her very closely, but he was also trying to invent a way to ask her to stay with him forever.

"Atoms, germs; they'll skew any little natural thing into a weapon. They see clouds, wind, rain, food, all the good things of their lives and they work late to make them dangerous. Where's the safe, warm place in that world, Mr. Loman?

"You guys live pretty well and those lies and fires I was talking about are even catching up with you. They're licking at your sky and you know it. That's why I'm here, isn't it?"

She felt tall, rangy, lonely like a hero. Her voice was steady like a person's voice. Not like something heard through a juice can, which is the way she always heard it before. They were listening. Vito noiselessly poured coffee, nodding his head again and again in secret accord.

"And you can stop worrying about TV," she said. "It has its moments, but most of it is not so great. Anyway it's not the problem. It's just a piece of it."

"Then what *is* the problem?" Moll asked impatiently.

"You've known all along what the problem is!" Roger was standing, shouting, startling them all and making his coffee cup dance panicky with a wild move of his arm. "And why not, I'd like to know? You sing about it every damn official opportunity that comes along!"

"Mr. Frommage! We'll have none of that here," Miss Havisham promised. "I'll thank you to lower your voice!"

"With all due respect to you, Miss Havisham, I will not! I may not be written, but I'm real as the rest of you and I will be heard."

Roger rocked with what he knew.

"Love! Trust! Imagination! Or rather the lack of such qualities. That's your problem." This last word was more brutal than Roger meant it to be. Its long aftertone sent a shiver through the crystal pears of the chandelier. Their melancholy tinkle seemed like a comment lightly raining on the diners.

"I'm just someone passed over and ignored. No one's seen fit to dream me up. No genius has dropped what they were doing to rush over to a desk and record me. Must I, a creature with a soul judged ineligible even to dress you for your dramatic parties—insufficient in grandeur even to deliver your fateful telegrams—must I tell you, with all your celebrity and vast experience, why you live again and again? Why you live at all?

"Isn't it to bear witness? To remind? To affirm the variety of human possibilities? To make sense out of their long and very short lives? Weren't you ordained to make those lives better?"

The characters were too shocked to answer. Mostly they were thinking, "Roger Frommage, of all people."

"He's right," Marina cried. "I know he is! That's what I wanted to tell you. That's what's going wrong. There's a terrible emptiness. Some of us are ashamed just for being old. We don't feel a part of anything.

"Ministers have lied to us," she gasped. "Presidents have lied to us! Generals are liars! Teachers lied! Doctors told us lies! Writers have told us lies!

"And for what?" she growled. "For power? Safety? For appliances? To keep that fire away? Anybody here got a good reason?"

Willy Loman wept. His tears plip-plopped tiny depressions into a half-eaten piece of cheesecake.

Athos cleared his throat. "I don't know why, Marina," he said in a mellow, weary way. "As you say, the world isn't simple. But what can be done about it now? Isn't it too late and way beyond us?"

Roger said no. "Please, Musketeer, whatever you do, don't sing me that one. That's the oldest kind of failure of the imagination and I don't believe it. I will not believe that I have spent the generations in stupefying tedium without ever getting so much as a crack at one lousy little great moment. Uh uh. No thank you to your nothing-can-be-done-about-it. I've heard that before. That's death."

"Amen," added Uncle Tom. "The least we can do is make some trouble."

"But where do we start?" Moll wondered.

"Here and now," Marina said firmly. "First we have to figure out what our resources are. Is there anything like an army or a police force here?"

"Sort of," Uncle Tom said. "But not exactly. A long time ago we tried to do something about those people who peek at the last page of a book before they've read it. It's very upsetting to end all of a sudden, out of the blue. Even if it's a happy ending. It shakes you up. It's jarring.

"Anyway, we rounded up some of the characters to form a squad to sqelch disorderly reading, but we couldn't figure out a way to make ourselves felt. So nothing much came of it. I've still got all the names and addresses, though."

"I'm sure that'll be very helpful," Marina said, doing her best to be convincing.

"I say we quit fooling around and go to Pearl." It was Anna Karenina. Out of the delicate ruby mouth placed in the perfect ivory face came these tough words.

But stepping out of character couldn't have been anything new to them. It would take just one inclement Sunday, whiled away playing gin with any King Henry unto bleariness, to rid even the most reverent of those kinds of illusions. And this they had done more than once.

No, it was the mere mention of an ordinary first name that brittled them and stiffened the air with a mystical charge. Marina felt the tension and found it hopeful. "Who's Pearl?" she asked.

"Pearl is just a short story," Moll snipped.

"The shortest," Athos added, pleasing himself and laughing in generous compensation for the others, who weren't.

Miss Havisham was restless. "It's time to get out of here. Vito has another party coming in and he has to clean up. I don't want to talk about Pearl. I don't want to talk about anybody. I just want to go home and take a nap."

She pushed herself away from the table with a great deal of effort, rising, raising a dismissing right hand. "We are adjourned. Thank you for your participation. Marina, nice to meet you. We'll meet again soon."

The group was silent, every eye on the spinster making her painstaking way to the exit. She moved with the caution of a woman whose passions had been absorbed and consumed by a lifetime of trying not to step on a train.

In the doorway she turned to them and spoke, "Until that time, I want you to remember that the best frame of mind is no frame at all."

VIII
KINDS OF FLOWERS

THE FAMOUS OLD LAMPLIGHTER was just starting work when Roger and Marina wandered out of Il Paradiso almost in a daze. This elderly man was so truly creased that the wrinkles of his skin ran unbroken into the wrinkles of his suit like rivers, scorning the notion of dominion, rushing from one territory to another. He stopped at each post, positioned his ladder, mounted, kindled and dismounted. He did this without variation or reference to the rest of the world as if, a long time ago, he'd joined them in thinking of himself as a silhouette.

By the light, Roger knelt down like a courtier and, taking her hand to kiss, he whispered, "Nice going, Mademoiselle de Queens. You really came true in there. On behalf of the unrevered and unrecorded of all the worlds' worlds, I bless you and offer you the biggest room in my heart. It's yours eternally, won so fair and square."

"Thanks, Roger." She felt triumphant and embarrassed. "I guess we did make quite a pair in there. It went so fast, I don't even know what I said."

"I do. You were ferocious and truthful. You shook them. Being important hasn't been good for their souls.

Once upon a time they were all regular guys. But the limelight fries it out of them. They like their privileges and they forget about desperation. They forget what it's like to wait. When they think about coffee, they're thinking who's going to bring it to them.

"Oh, but the way you told them off! Saint Joan could take a leaf or two from your book, and don't think she won't be hearing about it tonight when I see her."

"Tonight? Couldn't we just stay home tonight? I don't want to meet any more people right now, if that's okay with you."

"Sure, sure, I understand. You go home and take it easy. I won't be late. I want to make the rounds and be sure that the real story of what happened this afternoon gets heard."

"But the others can tell them," Marina said.

"That's what I'm afraid of. They'll tell it and each time they do, we'll get nastier and more unreasonable and they'll get wittier and more wise. Will you have any trouble getting home?"

"I don't think so. I'll be fine."

"You know the address. It's Number 24 War and Peace Way. If you get lost, ask someone or take a taxi. Here's some money. See you later."

Catching his sleeve to keep him from leaving, she waited until he was completely turned around to ask her question.

"Roger, who's Pearl?"

"I promise I'll tell you about her sometime soon. Not now, Marina. Tomorrow or the day after. When the time is right. Trust me."

"You know I do," she reassured nobody.

Roger was gone, in a hurry on a holy mission to bars. Before the evening was out he'd be buying the drinks and referring to her as "La Farina." He'd fold his white jacket carefully inside out over the back of a chair. And he'd dance because he was such a good dancer.

She looked at the money. It was a rectangle of silky paper with three hearts, a full moon on purple stars and a parrot chained to a stand, within a border of brown seashells. There was nothing to indicate how much it would buy or by whose authority it was money. It wasn't real. It wasn't fake. It was money.

The shabby Old Lamplighter's monotonous duties had taken him only a short distance, when Marina saw his lumpy back ahead of her, she wanted to rush past him with her eyes closed, but that would look funny and she had no reason to wish to offend him. It was the unrelenting evenness of his moving to light, to move again, that frightened her. His every action was too much like the previous one to be human.

Marina pulled herself tight together and walked by him as if he was a big dog sitting on a leash of unknown length. When she was nearest, he turned and grinned a hideous Harpo smile. Her heart slipped. There was something in his hand.

That hand came up slow in a creepy mechanical

giving arc. It was gnarled and liver-spotted, but better to look at than the face. In it was a printed business card. She took it without looking up, breathing, reading it or saying thank you.

When she was three blocks away she realized that she had no recollection of walking that distance. Stopping by an empty lot, she forced herself to look at the card. There was just enough day left to read it by.

It said, "For the ultimate experience in dining pleasure, Cafe Aurora Borealis." On the left side was a drawing of a polar bear holding a cocktail shaker high in both paws. There were little whirr lines around the shaker to suggest vibration. Beneath the bear it said, "Singles Coddled." Below that, "Your Home Away from Home." And there was an address.

Marina grew easy and laughed. She turned the card over. On the other side, written in the round, earnest longhand of a high school girl, "Make them tell you about Pearl. And don't be frightened. Please."

She toyed with the idea of waiting for the Lamplighter to catch up with her, but that would take forever so she started walking home.

Marina window-shopped and that was great fun because every style was still in style in In The Beginning. Much Ado About Nothing Boulevard was their Fifth Avenue. It was a broad mall dotted with sandstone urns of evergreens and bulbs. The windows were witty tableaus about butter or leather or whatever they were offering.

She was enchanted by the mechanized window of a

toga shop. Pompeii bustled in fanatic detail. Ancient dentists stood outside their establishments, appreciating the day. Archaic beauticians and minor officials went about their business on concealed tracks. Dolphins bobbed and frolicked in the chartreuse Bay of Naples. Vesuvius cast a cool, relieving shadow over the busy city, puffing pink smoke that rose and joined the pastel sky.

She had never seen anything like it until she turned around and caught some lamplight tripping off the sparkles in the spines of the two basalt panthers that were the imposing front doors to the headquarters of Cathay Trading. Marina went right up to them and pushed hard on their nacre handles. The doors rolled open. Cathay Trading was never closed.

Before her was a long green glass arcade. She could see a man seated at a writing desk at the other end. He looked up from his work and smiled and waved her to come to him. Her skin went "oooh" on the way because it was like walking through an emerald.

"Thank you," he said. He was wearing a simple cotton night-black robe, plain, except for a couple of stars. His hair, his face, his hands, his whole appearance was smooth, as if he'd been worked on for a long time by a strong wind in a very high place.

"Thank you," he repeated. "It's a rare blessing when delight comes looking for you. Cinnabar, fireworks, a charm; anything you say, just as soon as I finish copying this out."

In less than a minute he was looking up again and smiling.

"What does it say?" Marina asked.

"I who was given in a dream the brush of many colors wish to write on petals a message to the clouds of morning."

"My name is Pao Yu," he said, offering her his hand. What'll it be?"

"Fireworks," Marina said.

"An excellent choice!" said Pao Yu. "Come with me. For this we'll need the Dome of Heaven. It's very near and on the way we can decide which series you'll take."

"What are my choices?"Marina asked as they passed through a sapphire corridor.

"Infinite," he said, shaking his head and laughing in awe. "But my instincts tell me that you would enjoy 'Kinds of Flowers.'"

"It sounds just right," she agreed.

They stopped at a simple ivory door.

"On the other side of this door is night," he cautioned. "Hold my hand."

When they were inside, Pao Yu announced, "Kinds of Flowers."

Instantly, a rumbling deep thunder-pack ripped through the darkness, convincing Marina that there was no floor and that the room was limitless.

She was trying to catch her breath when a swarm of sizzling garnets shot out of the void and bloomed into fat pink fiery peonies. They lasted a few seconds and were replaced by chrysanthemums, round icebergs with stunning carmine wounds; then a shower of creamy jasmine and lilac florets, then murky plum orchids with mauve folds, and gaping velvet-eyed anemones collared by primary blues and reds, and a fleece of gardenias with toasted centers, and cool, lemon freesia, and hearty copper camellias and hibiscus with flaming stamens and roses, too.

Marina was squeezing Pao Yu's hand so tightly that he thought perhaps she'd had enough. He pulled her through the plain door and through the topaz hall to the front entrance.

"Come back any time and see more," he said. "They say the peacocks and flamingos in 'Kinds of Birds' are not easily forgotten."

Marina felt certain that the fact that she was unable to speak didn't bother him at all.

The Merchant of Venice was just locking up for the night as Marina passed by and he asked her if she wanted a ride home. On the way she told him her story and they both marvelled at how imaginative life can be. Before he dropped her off he chided her for not dressing warmly enough for the time of year. This is pneumonia weather," he told her. "One nice day and you kids run around like it's summer. And then you can't understand why you get sick." She loved being scolded by him.

During the day, Roger's amaryllis had grown top heavy and clattered from the night table to the floor. When

Marina got back, she picked up the blossom and the chards and wrote him a note. Then she went to sleep.

Roger returned at dawn, wide awake and humming. The day's events made him interesting. Characters, the kind that had always pretended not to see him when he entered a room, had fallen over themselves trying to entice him to sit at their tables. They wanted his opinions. Even the sacred March sisters were giving him sticky come-hither looks. Jude the Obscure tried to tell him a joke–"A rabbi and a priest were walking down the street . . ."–but there were too many interruptions.

He found her message forked on a sailor figurine. "Dear Roger, I'm going to sleep. Your plant fell over. She grew too big to live in a pot. I couldn't find a vacuum. I did the best I could. Love, Marina."

"And how would she know if she *had* found a vacuum?" Roger wondered as he scanned the pantry for something good to eat.

IX

AND I ONLY AM ESCAPED ALONE TO TELL THEE

RAMONA DIAMANT COULDN'T come to the phone. Its ringing sliced up the still air that a moment earlier had carried only frisbees and light vollyball cries through the open windows of Madison, Wisconsin.

The Pequod and the Whale were swallowed up; Ishmael floated on a flat, undangerous sea. The telephone continued to shrill like an unhappy baby or a dog, reaffirming its anguish with the loony concentration of creatures that can't resort to synonyms.

The Rachel claimed Ishmael, freeing him to knock off and go home. Ramona assessed her own chances of being rescued and determined that they were sorrowfully slim. There was just another half ring and she reluctanly disembarked from the myth, giving in to what she thought of as a Japanese emotion.

It was a powerful longing, so wide and unordinary that its oceanic sadness made her feel alive and that made her almost happy and then miserable again.

Ramona wasn't at home anywhere. She felt like a spy in life and the ending of every great book and each orgasm, and the sight of every homeless shopping bag lady infected her with a titanic yearning for the world to make an unscheduled stop.

When she made love she could see history to the tune of Beethoven's logical thunder, a fabulous documentary of restored umbilical cords, revealing the most agonizing connections, stringing her and everything the world has seen on a necklace of the generations that threaded itself back all the way through the crawly, tentative land dwellers to those one-celled jewels near the clasp.

A friend told her that we are made of the same gas and information that make comets. She scrutinized every lover, every writer, every bus driver, everyone, for signs of telltale dazzle that might mean they were potential coconspirators, possible companions on the exhausting machete trek back through experience to something true, or at least, important.

But where were they? The people she knew gave philosopher's names to their big dogs. They had quick, this-time-it's-for-keeps affairs with new religions and they gave a great deal of thought to selecting imported cheeses and special African coffees.

She studied the tall boys with the beautiful chests and the heavy Mexican buckles that must have hurt them when they bent down, and she wondered what they could be thinking.

When the war was over they simmered down. When nothing changed quickly their response was to move to the country.

Once they were for large, sprawling families and then they didn't want any families at all. They loved clothes and then they didn't. Their orbits decayed, becoming more frantic and personal, until they had only themselves to circle. They were so easily had with such modest expectations.

If their new gods or their old gods could see, they would raise the roofs off the red brick cottages and find that the only things still working were the sleek German coffee grinders in kindergarten colors, grinding out good taste. Everything else was out of order and they couldn't understand why they couldn't get along.

"And I Only Am Escaped Alone To Tell Thee," Ramona repeated out loud until she was wailing.

"One is enough," she promised herself. "I have to do something. A book about a person like me. Every word must be a wake-up call to workers and inheritors, the lucky and the unlucky, both. They're going to read my book and remember what they have in common with comets. They're going to see themselves when they see the stars. And when they're through reading, they won't be sure if they've dreamt it or not. But it won't matter, because it will be in the world to make trouble, to make them feed each other."

She glared at a plastic bottle of herbal shampoo and threw it across the room, knowing that it was sealed tight and that, for the moment, this was an anger without consequences.

X
YAMA

MARINA AND ROGER SAT on a bench under a willow tree in Middlemarch Park, eating roast beef on rye with Russian dressing while the birds ate Nancy Drew. The birdseed statue of the young investigator wore a miter of bickering cardinals atop her short curls. Jays perched and snacked on her left arm which ended in a gloved hand, cupped to her ear to better hear some faint, perilous sound. Robins, wanting no trouble, roosted like hassled refugees on the flashlight held in her other hand. They were careful not to provoke the attention of the feisty cardinals and jays. They chose instead to face the nearby hills that were covered with healthy, fat green trees, standing like tightly packed broccoli.

Roger and Marina savored their sandwiches and the sunlight that came filtered through the mysteries of bird organization as the broad osier branches stroked the sweet air as if in an attempt to put the park to sleep. A couple of foggy, party-filled days and nights had melted together and passed away since the battle of the Italian restaurant, and Marina was fed up with hors d'oeuvres and introductions.

"I don't want to cause any problems," she said, tight-lipped, trying to conceal the rye bread that wadded up around her teeth. "But this is the last time I'm asking you about Pearl. No more excuses and no more 'laters.' I mean it, Roger. I've got to know."

Roger didn't look at Marina. "She hurt us very badly. I didn't like putting you off, but I didn't know what to tell you."

"Just tell me what you know."

"It was long ago," he said, tilting his head to find the sun, "before there were holes in our sky . . . before we became confused.

"Pearl was young, friendly and beautiful in a strange, sneaky way. She had a wonderful, anxious body that was always in some kind of motion. You wanted to quiet her down, but that was foolish. She was made like a hummingbird.

"Her eyes were large and far apart and they beamed shameless curiosity. She couldn't be made to avert them. But no perfect, classical features.

"Maybe she never knew how lovely she was, but men did. They'd pass her on the street and one glimpse had a terrible, long half-life. She'd reoccur to them for days. They'd forget what they were doing, because as Mr. Blake would've surely observed if he'd had the good fortune to run into her, she'd planted herself in their nerves.

"But you must remember, it wasn't anything obvious. There was nothing easy about her."

Gorged birds departed, making graceless flights to the hills. Hungry birds replaced them.

"From the start, we knew she was a main character. Pearl was too crazy, too rare, too finely drawn to be a lady-in-waiting or a roommate. We assumed that someone very talented was writing her and the readers would know her in the same troubled way that we did.

"I remember waking up in the middle of the night in a cold sweat. 'What is my life?' I wondered. The answer came lonely and anonymous, and it made me afraid of the sound of my own heart.

"All I had to calm me was the possibility, the fantasy that I might be in Pearl's book. I got through a lot of clammy darkness dreaming up a situation that we might share. A mutual adventure that might conclude with her loving me or being grateful. At the time I would've liked that better than being Hamlet. But it didn't turn out that way."

"You mean she wasn't written?" Marina asked from inside the trance of the narrative.

"No, she was," he assured her, touched by her seriousness. "She was written very well, and until now we thought it must be the worst thing that ever happened to us."

"But, why? I don't understand. I thought being written was like money in the bank. I thought that's what you live for."

"Well, never having had any money in the bank, I couldn't say what that's like. But, you're right, it's what we live for."

"Then what went wrong? You said she was well written."

"Yes, she was. Pearl moved through the pages as she moved through our lives—quick, smart and hard on the memory. The author caught her in all her troubled glory. But it was like watching a snowball."

"I don't get it," Marina complained.

"You will, if you listen. No more questions, please. I'm telling you a sad story.

"The book was called *Yama*, which means 'the heights' in Japanese and 'the depths' in Russian. This was a good title because it was a book about heaven and hell.

"It began in a fabulous, stuffy living room in Upstate New York on New Year's Eve in 1900, just around midnight. There were several servants, but only two celebrants: a naturalist and the mistress of the first advertising executive.

"'The twentieth century will not be a good one for birds,' the naturalist warned over champagne. His name was John and he told Olive, the mistress, that sturgeon were disappearing from the sullied Hudson and the skies were smudged with the ash of business. He said that the new age came with 'the edges of a smothering blanket between its meager fingers.' And that when it was over, the world would be struggling and clawing for breath from beneath a wasteful haze.

"Olive suffered from asthma, a mostly nocturnal disorder. The best doctors gave her useless drops the color of amethysts. She transferred them to Lalique perfume bottles, shaped like lilies and swans.

"Like some misinformed vampire, she passed her too long, wheezy nights, withdrawn, no matter who was there. She prayed for the dawn that brought air and rest as if she were allergic to darkness, rather than feathers and dust. As if her lungs were sensitive to light. She was vibrant in the afternoon and mad for the company of intelligent, healthy people. She'd flare again at dinnertime and tell daring, provocative lies to keep her guests from leaving. She'd do anything to make them stay.

"Progress was the big deal in those days. Mass production. But the night is a special kind of factory; it can't be modernized.

"When Olive heard the naturalist's prognosis for the new century it affected her personally. Perhaps better than anyone, she could appreciate, in a sleepless, physical way, what the destruction of the international respiratory system would be like. She pleaded with John to use his popular brain to prevent such a disaster. He told her he'd think about it. Three shades of sherbet were served and they toasted the last hundred years with the bravado that passed for humor among the rich and unreflective people of that age.

"But they knew they were in trouble. They lived at odds with the rhythm and spin of the earth and their absurd amounts of money were merely a means of living in the steeply mortgaged past. And this they could not accomplish completely.

"The present and the future intruded into their salons and laundries. Working people gathered to share rage against these effortless lives in reassembled castles. Even the artists, whom they imported from Europe and treated as if they were their own children, repaid them with discordant, unpretty music that sounded like machines. They made paintings of fruit that you would never think was real. No one in his right mind would want to eat that fruit.

"They took the industrial symphonies and the funhouse images and they framed them in the gilt of old beauty. But there was something wrong. There were gaslights in their submarines.

"John returned on Twelfth Night to tell Olive what he planned. He wanted her to purchase a vast tract of land in the Hudson Valley so that he might try his hand at paradise. He'd given it a great deal of thought and he had decided that the only solution was to build a hotel. This didn't make perfect sense to Olive, but money was water and she needed sensations, so building began in the spring.

"Of course, the first thing they made was a wall, a thick, tall wall out of rocks from Japan. And they made seven imperial pagodas out of these same rocks. I don't know why they had to go so far to get the rocks, and I have no idea why there were seven. Maybe because it's a powerful number, or maybe because they thought they needed that many. Who knows? Who's left to care?

"Those seven moody giants cast a lot of shade. They

enforced a perpetual dusk upon the oriental gardens of dwarfed, flaming trees and implausibly arched moon bridges that spanned the trout-choked, black-green brooks like anxious cats.

"But it wasn't all dark. There was a lighthearted pink New Orleans street with lace balconies. And a long, glass art gallery, inspired by a recent exposition. And a white library stuffed with first editions, including an original folio and a Bible in Mary Baker Eddy's own hand. It was open every one of the twenty-four hours.

"The residence was like a great house gone to a masquerade ball. Its ruse was Versailles and it was more like what it pretended to be than its inspiration ever was. It contained a hundred bedrooms with a hundred historical beds. I, personally, consider all beds to be historic. To tell you the truth, I'd feel a lot better if everyone did. But these particular old beds were supposed to be important because of the great dreams they had once supported. People like Ivan the Terrible and Abraham Lincoln—you get the picture—had tossed and turned in them.

"Each room had its own theme, its own Carrara masterpiece and no room was like another down to the weave of the washcloth.

"You could've convened the congress of any industrial power within the walls of the dining room. The freezer, alone, was appropriate for treaty signing. It was lined with ancient Dutch tiles of seas and mills in impossible blues and appointed with brass and oak. The dining room was scrupulously grand, except for one bizarre and disturbing feature, a much larger than life bronze of a howling wolf that dominated the cavernous hearth, eying the diners and projecting a superior notion of appetite. When the fire roared, the beast appeared to do the same. Consequently, guests were highly specific about their seating requests, preferring to confront the torches of the metal sconces that gleamed like weapons.

"The naturalist's specifications had been faithfully executed to the most eccentric letter and Yama was ready to open on a burnished spring day in 1905. The Japanese ambassador attended in tails, his narrow chest traversed by a vermillion Miss America sash. It was his honor to cut the ceremonial ribbon, perhaps, because they'd bought so many of his rocks. It's hard to say.

"A visit to Yama was by invitation only, and those honored on that halcyon day were people with a big piece of the national imagination. Henry Ford, Thomas Edison and Rosa O'Neill, the designer of the kewpie doll launched together on that first day. And Pearl sectioned their grapefruits.

"Mr. Edison was attempting to describe his new motion picture machine. He wanted to build a theatre for it, but he hadn't known where to put it, until he came to Yama. Mr. Ford wasn't getting the drift. He changed the subject to afterlife.

"Olive sent a much re-written invitation to Mark Twain. She was anticipating the best dinner conversation of her life, but when Twain arrived, his old bones thoroughly rattled by an attenuated trip through the mountains, he realized it was not for him and he checked out, leaving his daughter Maria, and her husband, Ossip, the conductor, to make his excuses. Olive tried to content herself with the company of James Montgomery Flagg, purveyor of Uncle Sam.

"Pearl rinsed the fruitcup stickiness from her chapped hands and budged open one of the massive kitchen doors. Through the crack, she watched the steel men, the bankers, the railroad barons, the senators, the builders, the judges, the annunciators of the country's crudest prejudices, and she damned the man who forgot to invite the anarchist.

"But the naturalist was delighted with his creation. He conceived it to require little, beyond its luminaries from the unreliable outside world. If the elsewhere were to shrivel up, the guests would have to forego only their coffee and pepper.

"Yama was a great success. Edison watched with pride as the awkward shadows curtsied across the screen in his movie theater. It was his idea to engrave 'ALL THE WORLD'S A STAGE' above the entrance. Olive savored the company of the mighty, who, like herself, had difficulty falling asleep. And Pearl made designs out of lemons and limes, until one steamy evening, she was discovered wandering the grounds in her honest, gray uniform by a young Rockefeller or a Frick. I can't remember. Anyway, he couldn't be dissuaded and they honeymooned at Saratoga, flaunting the unlikelihood of their love as if it were one of Mr. Ford's deluxe models.

"Yama lasted until the crash. It closed soon after, its economics no longer practical. Olive lived on there with a caretaker and a blind writer, until some time later it was purchased by ten black families in the insurance and undertaking businesses. They, too, thought that they could find peace in isolation, but it didn't work for them either. They sold the little world to a man who turned it into a summer camp. He sold it to the Mafia. They tore down the fantasy buildings to make way for the trailers of the workers at a nearby pharmaceuticals factory. Olive was very old when she died. Very crisp and old, leaving the local Women's Auxiliary the most fabulous collection of absolutely lifelike porcelain birds."

"Jesus," Marina said. "Sounds like a bestseller to me.

"It would've been if it hadn't been for Pearl. But she wouldn't go after the first read and that was that."

"What do you mean, she wouldn't go? How could she not?"

"Why don't you ask her yourself? She lives out in the suburbs with the stereotypes. It's only a commuter's ride away. I'll get you a schedule." Roger stood up and brushed the crumbs away. "Yes, you should go out there and meet her. You'll like each other. You've both got spunky hearts."

"Will you come with me, Roger?"

"No, I couldn't do that. Some things live better in the memory." He rubbed his eyes. "Mostly those things that never really lived at all. But give her my best. You can tell her that we still think about her. That would be true."

"Roger, why haven't you been written?"

"Because, honey, character ain't destiny."

"Don't joke. I want to know."

"I don't know myself," he confessed. "I just don't seem to be what they have in mind. I only wish I knew if I missed my time or if it hasn't come yet."

"One more question," she said as they collected the luncheon refuse. "What did the naturalist hope to accomplish with Yama? What kind of difference did he want it to make?"

"He never did say."

They passed the empty pedestal where Nancy Drew no longer stood. The girl detective had been devoured down to her pumps. The cardinals, jays and robins had flown away to the thickness of the hills, taking all her clues and solutions with them.

XI
SACRIFICE FLIES

HAMLET WAS DECISIVE AND he knew all the words by heart.

"Oh, this is my favorite song! Won't you dance with me? You must! Your answer is 'yes' and I promise you weightlessness." He placed his fully open hand firmly against Marina's ribs. They felt so thin. "Marina, are you an ocean inside?" he wondered. "Are your ribs brilliant-colored like the unseen aerial coral that tats itself amongst the secrets of the sea?" He pushed her through the smoking and drinking restaurant crowd and the back door into the unused garden.

Hamlet flicked a switch and the slender trees dotted up with vague cocktail onion lights. Marina and Hamlet danced to the remnants of a favorite song, which was "They Can't Take That Away From Me," and then to the six favorite songs that followed. It was the first hot night of the year. The slate stepping stones, which their feet hardly touched, perspired slightly, enticing little moss fingers to come closer.

Ishmael watched them through a cloudy window. At home in his loneliness, he was trying to imagine how they looked to each other. He was trying to remember what he once felt about Pearl. He was fishing for the props and mirrors of another summer night. But nothing was coming.

"They CAN take that away from me," he joked with himself. "Time can take anything and sooner or later it does. It's a great eater, efficient like the shark, and it eats sharks, too. We cannot get a hold of time."

Hamlet and Marina waltzed past the dirty window that had been looked through rarely since it was new. She was telling him that it was her birthday. Ishmael saw them as one body. The ice in his bourbon had melted and the outside of the glass was slippery. "Moisture," he silently toasted, "you are the dearest blessing. The unmixed blessing and the means to all others. The very dearest."

Hamlet was telling Marina that there was a birthday party at his apartment, when he disappeared during the ides of "September Song." Marina looked around and felt as if she'd been slapped hard and unexpectedly in the face.

"It's a read," Ishmael explained from the doorway. "He just had to go. He really couldn't help it. Let me get you a drink."

"Please," she answered in a recuperative tone of voice. "It threw me for a minute. I wasn't prepared. I don't like vanishing. Come to think of it, I'm not wild about goodbyes, either. A friend once told me that separations are dreams. Of course, he was on his way to the coast at the time. Can I have a glass of cold white wine?"

"Sure. Why don't you pull two chairs together outside? We'll get ripped and we'll shoot the flimsy land breeze. Hamlet will be back before you know it. It's probably just some student wringing out a last minute paper on "The Experience of Doubt in Shakespeare" or "Texture in the Tragedies" or something like that. Nothing serious. We'll get plowed and he or she will fall asleep and then you'll be reunited with your Prince."

When Ishmael returned with a glass and a bottle of wine, Marina was waiting with a question. "What's out there, Ishmael?"

"How far out do you wish to go?"

"Not so far. Just to the suburbs."

"That's farther than you realize," he replied. The bourbon was settling all through him, giving him the impression that his nervous system could be understood as an electronic Paris subway map. "I push the button coordinates for will and action," he reasoned, "and the way, the way most direct and true from the one to the other, will be lit and easily taken."

"Yes, yes. I'm sure you're right about the suburbs, but, that's not what I'm asking. I want to know who lives out there." From the corner of her eye, Marina thought she saw a firefly. With shooting stars and fireflies, in all matters of momentary illumination, the speed of disbelief approaches the speed of light. She scanned the garden for another sighting.

"What's suddenly so interesting about the suburb?" he asked.

"No special reason," she answered, defensively. "I just would like to know who's out there."

"Who's out there, my angel, are aging beauties and unrequited thousandaires. It's a real paradise for nosy neighbors, noisy neighbors, city mice, country mice, sympathetic prostitutes, tight-assed socialites, lecherous ministers, lusty grenadiers, embittered academics, slighted clerks, larcenous guardians, mechanics' mechanics and nuns with buns.

"They see the world through blue eyes that turn gray at the sight of trouble. And they want some things so bad they can taste them.

"Their mothers are either perfect or cruel. Their fathers, corduroyed or drunk.

"If they happen to be Japanese, they will fold paper, they will garden or they will kill themselves to be polite. The Germans among them will be having science and dark fun. The Italians will cook and hug and racketeer. The Latins won't wear watches. The Irish will weep.

"The Blacks will get into trouble, or else, years later the call will come from Stockholm or Washington and they'll hurry there with gray temples and shallow commas in their palms where the fingernails have done the digging.

"The Protestants will not tell each other how they feel. And the Jews will never stop telling everyone how they feel. They will never stop and they're clever.

"That's what you'll find out there. Lanes with the names of trees and no surprises. Don't move." Ishmael ran inside for more bourbon and returned in time to reclaim the cadence of his soliloquy with no need for a "where was I?"

"You see, my gorgeous friend, I believe in Incarnation. In-car-na-tion! The one life, that can be enough, lived in the risky upper case with a maximum of embarrassment. I hate the sentences that telegraph on ahead how they'll be ending. I loathe the stories that end locked in cheap rhyme with their beginnings. Womb to tomb. Womb to tomb. Birth to earth. Things happen in between. Shattering things!

"Great waves come up, great fish. Our stars are not where we last admired them. Our homes crumble and we don't know which place to long for. The course must be changeable and vast. The charts, the tales can be no less. Not a current left out. Not a reef.

"The words must be used with care. Not cheaply, not falsely, because they derive their value, their meaning from ages of violent collisions and daring tenderness. I say the process is not finished either. I despise the stereotypes because they deaden our senses. Because they are never more or less than they appear to be.

"But Pearl lives with them. Why?"

"I will not speak of Pearl."

"Alright, don't. Then tell me why Uncle Tom doesn't."

"I said stereotypes, damn it, not archetypes!" The mention of Pearl's name had hit him hard. He had to ask himself whether or not he'd been railing at her, rather than a mass of tired images. But he was so thoroughly tight, he forgot to answer. He did know that he had no real quarrel with Marina. He resolved to be softer.

"I know what you mean about stereotypes, but aren't there any fixtures in life? Aren't there some things that happen to all of us? Things that we share with all human beings?"

"Yes. Sure. All human beings and some animals. There's love and lost love and illness and triumph and death, of course. These are the ports and lighthouses. But we come to them in unique ways with exceptional baggage."

"Lighthouses," she murmured. "I've been thinking about lighthouses and a woman I never knew, but only heard about afterwards. She met her husband in graduate school. They were two scientists. The only married couple in the world capable of measuring the light from lighthouses. This odd job took them everywhere. And then one Sunday morning while she was still young and he was still asleep, she walked into the neglected garden of a rented house and blew her brains out. No note.

"Now this is a story that can be told quickly. But the life, itself, took much longer. I've wondered in waiting rooms and taxis where that thing which lies between the living and the telling can be found."

Ishamel had nothing to say. He had too much to think. They watched the fireflies. Marina rose as if her name had been called.

"I'm going to see Pearl. I just have to. I know you don't approve of her. Nobody around here does. But I have to find something out. You should understand that, you of all sailors."

"I do." He was keeping his eyes on the bugs. "Does Roger know you're going?"

"I told him that I would. But I think he thinks I'm going tomorrow. He left the house in a hurry, said something about shagging flies."

"Shagging flies? Oh yes, for the big baseball game tomorrow. Oh Roger, Roger. Every year, every lonely, unrecorded year he practices and practices for that game. He wears himself out. He dreams of unassisted triple plays and the cheering pats of his grateful teammates. And when it's time to pass out bats and mitts they don't even see him. Passed over, every year. They won't even let him sit in the dugout.

"So he sits in the stands, recording every sneeze on his scorecard and telling anyone who'll listen how lovely it all is. Telling them that the baseball diamond refracts the unhandled mysteries of space for the sake of us poor mites. It's a way for us to see the universe, just as we, ourselves, are a means for the universe to see itself."

Marina bent down to kiss Ishmael goodbye. He pulled the short sleeves of her tee shirt closer to him for a harder kiss.

"You see," he told the last firefly, when they were alone, "we're more than we know."

XII
SILVERED ALMONDS

THE DOEVILLE ZEPHYR WAS a fine red train. Its name was written on all thirteen cars in a gold cloisonne, so intricate and natural, it could have been shaved from the sides of a prize aquarium fish. The cars, themselves, might have been joined together by a jeweler. Their tops were rounded and sleeked with jolts of black enamel lightning. At this late hour, waiting in the station for the night's last trip, the Doeville Zephyr, like a ruby bracelet lying open on a bureau dresser, suggested great events.

Marina found a seat in a compartment with a ferret-faced woman absorbed in a "How To Draw Cats" book and another lady who folded and refolded a large map-of-Texas scarf. When the train began to move, Marina gave them both light opening smiles, but there was no reaction. She trailed a finger down the ribs and raised DZ's of the amber short-haired velvet upholstery and looked out the window at fleeting trees and laundry.

Transportation always made her happy. Riding along in someone else's automobile, she would keep to her own side, sucking in the sights and forced air from a vent, quiet and occupied like a baby.

It was during these times that she told herself that she was really living. Her secret assignment was fascination. It was her job to pretend that she was from somewhere else; another planet where there were no houses, cows, bridges or lilies. She tried to pull assumptions and familiarities out of herself like a magician. It was the price she paid to be in love with the world; to erase the numbers and reconnect the dots in the truest and most beautiful pattern.

Marina meant to go sailing inside that found constellation. She intended to cruise to its heart, dropping fear and loneliness over the side, where it would never stop falling away from her.

That particular moment, as the Zephyr pulled into Doeville Station, Marina felt intensely alone. She clasped her hands for the brief moment when the fingers fool each other. She saw a conductor on the platform and decided to approach him for directions.

"Excuse me. Do you know the way to Pearl's house?"

"Yep."

Marina couldn't tell if it was a word or a hiccough. He had gray hair and he wore a musty navy blue uniform. His gold-trimmed glasses were low on his nose. He peered over them at an onion-shaped, stainless-steel pocket watch. Marina suspected he knew the time.

"Well, do you think you could tell me how to get there?"

"Yep." He started to walk away.

"HOW?"

"Three blocks straight. Make a right at the Post Office. Two more blocks. Left at the pharmacy. Down Plain Jane Lane. Number 66."

"Thanks. Why couldn't you just tell me that in the first place?"

"Doing my job," he droned. "It's all there in the contract. I was taken on as a middle-aged, taciturn son-of-a-bitch New England train conductor. They weren't hiring irresponsible, loveable Irish poets that day."

"It's your job to act that way? It's hard to believe."

"Hard and unnecessary. Or maybe you don't know where you are? This is Doeville. Best to remember."

No. 66 was a white clapboard house with evergreen trim and shutters, flowers, a driveway, no fence. The doorbell chimed the first few notes of "Auld Lang Syne" as Marina shifted from foot to foot in search of the best stance for a good impression. A Venetian blind slat moved out of its place and then back again and Marina could feel someone coming.

It was clear to Marina that the woman who opened the door wide was worthy of a decade of Ishmael's tossing and turning. She had the white, white teeth, honey skin and floppy, sable hair that make for round-the-clock prettiness. Marina could imagine Pearl waking up in the morning, sitting up, unfurling her napkin and smiling confidently at an enchanted man with a breakfast tray. She was female like a doe. She wore a fresh blue checked smock and crushed slippers. Marina was anxious to give her anything she wanted.

"What brings you to me, Cookie?" she asked warmly.

"I'm Marina from In The Beginning!", she cried. "Well, not really. Actually, I'm really from Queens. But one morning, the strangest of my life, I found myself there and I met Roger, who thinks about you , and Ishmael, who does, too, only he won't admit it. Your name made everyone so uncomfortable, I knew you must be something. I've come for your advice. I don't know if you know this, but things back in town are sort of dire. The sky is all screwed up and I want to go home. And Roger still hasn't been . . ."

"Written." Pearl supplied the verb and her hands in one gracious sweep. She pulled Marina through the doorway, designated a badly patched brown chenille chair as the most comfortable one in the living room and disappeared into the kitchen to telephone cancellations to her tiresome dinner guests. In ten minutes she was back, carrying iced tea with mint leaves. She sank down on the sofa and sighed. "I think of them both. I have lively conversations with them in my heart. But I'm afraid they were very angry with me when I left and they never understood.

"Marina, you're welcome here. Please tell me everything about my home. Have they been maintaining the statues? Is Miss Havisham still in charge? Is she well? Is she read? Does Bartleby still give those endless slideshows? Can you get a decent bowl of minestrone at Il Paradiso?"

Marina couldn't tell her adventures and impressions fast enough for Pearl. She was ravenous for what they wore and whom they were with. When the Horatio Alger delivery boy from Meats and Treats arrived with some groceries, Pearl rudely stuffed some uncounted money in his hand and almost pushed him out the door. "Don't leave anything out, Marina. Remember where you were," she instructed, returning to the deep, toasty impression she'd made in the sofa.

It was the middle of the night before she thought about eating. She asked Marina to accompany her to the kitchen so that they could keep talking while she cooked dinner. When Pearl opened a small paper sack she shook her head and laughed.

"Oh no. Not silvered almonds. I said slivered almonds. I wanted slivered almonds to go with the trout. I tell you, Marina, it's the revenge of the 'l' in almonds. He gets work so seldom (people say ahmonds) he's conspired with his brother 'i' to wreck my recipe. Plain trout's what you get when you offend a letter."

"I used to have trouble with salmon," Marina confessed. "And there's another word I can't handle. It started one summer night when I was a kid. I was very nervous and skinny and I was sitting with my father on aluminum folding chairs in front of our house. I was mad about him. Thanks to him I've spent most of my life in love. Not many people had air conditioners yet, so the neighborhood kept its doors and windows open and some people sat outside.

"He had a Sunday crossword puzzle on his lap. I think I was eight—eight or nine—and so glad to have him all to myself for an hour. I prayed that nobody else would come near us and I tried hard to think of smart things to say. He would answer and drift back into his puzzle.

"Then he pointed to the stars and said, as if we had been talking about stars, that some of them weren't really there anymore. That the light we saw was millions of years old. That it took so long to come to us that some of those stars were already dead.

"What an idea! I was helpless. He'd made me curious. He'd made the stars real places. I loved him so much that minute in his short-sleeved white shirt that smelled faintly of the city and the world's opening up. 'Oh Daddy, this thing about the stars,' I said, throwing my arms around his neck, 'isn't it morantic!'

"'You said it!' he told me, kissing me all over my face. 'Morantic! That's just what it is.'"

Pearl chopped onions for the salad. Marina was high and tired from so much talking. She emptied the bag of silvered almonds and studied them. They were like crazy nickels minted by a dream. She could see her reflection, squashed chubby and defenseless, the way it is in car fenders. En route to the refrigerator, Pearl joined Marina for a look at the nuts.

"A little cupping of the hands to sleep," Pearl mumbled. "That's from the Bible. It's so secretive, so personal, but I can't imagine what it means. I mean I could imagine it, but I can't know it. Can you?"

"No," Marina answered, unwilling to exchange her present thoughts for a new question. "But don't these nuts seem like magic?"

"They are magic. I can see things in them."

"Things besides us and the light fixture?"

"Yes." Pearl was concentrating on the nuts so hard it made Marina's hands tremble. She was afraid of upsetting them so she meditated on the opal veins in the formica counter. The thicker ones became rivers and where they branched she put cities. Then Pearl covered Marina's hands with her own and closed her eyes.

"Great forces," she proclaimed, her eyes shut tight, "forces as great as the ones that made the sky will mend the sky. Roger will have his heart's desire. It's closer than he knows. And you, Marina, are where you were meant to be. Let's eat."

"Eat? I can't eat. I have to know what you mean. Why am I here?"

"That's the big question of your lonely century." Pearl moved to the stove to lower a flame. "Maybe every century. But hot food turns cold too fast, so take my word for it; you are here and you will be . . . "

"Written?" As soon as Marina said it she heard it and her arm flew up like a catapult, sending the silvered almonds spraying across the room. Her throat stopped working and her nerves flashed urgent heaving messages to her brain. Her brain was clenched on "Written! Written! Written!"

"I was never anywhere else?" she shrieked. "Queens was just a dream? Family? Sex? School? Never was?" she gagged. "Never was? My friends, their secrets, I never had them? I never happened?"

"Of course you did! Marina, you must calm down. It's not the way you think it is. Not at all. Whatever happened to you was real. It's pieces of real time and space. Oh, honey, let me help."

The rage left Marina flat. She exhaled and sleepwalked out of the room. Pearl gathered tissues and a glass of water and followed her.

She found Marina cheek-to-cheek with the picture window. She was breathing on the glass. Over and over she fingerpainted her initials in the vapor.

"I brought you tissues and water," Pearl whispered. She took Marina's hand and placed it against her chest. "Is that real? Am I real?" Marina didn't do anything.

Pearl attempted a hug but there was nothing coming back and Marina's stiffness made her feel like a seal. She retreated to the kitchen to hide and make coffee. Marina appeared just as the water was boiling.

"If you're so crazy about your home town," Marina asked, "how come you don't live there?"

"I broke the law. Coffee?"

"Yes, please. Milk and sugar. But why? Why did you break the law?"

"Because I just had to."

"I need more than a 'just had to,'" Marina protested. "A 'just had to' won't help me," she said. "Pearl, tell me why you wouldn't be in that book."

"Because somebody said they were going to make it into a TV movie."

"No, really," Marina pleaded. "Why?"

"Well, as a matter of fact," she replied very slowly, "I did it for you."

"Now wait a . . . "

"Don't worry," Pearl said, waving her hands and feeling let down by human caution. "I didn't mean you personally; just whoever came after. The milk is in a pitcher with a pelican on it in the refrigerator. Come sit down, we'll have our coffee and I'll tell you about the day I was finished.

"A perfect day," she began when they were settled. "It had everything; light, warmth, birds, blue. I remember racing down the street that day in a short little dress that came from Haiti and dangerously high heels with grosgrain straps that tied around my ankles. I felt like a dish, but I felt strong, too. I was in flight.

"I thought I'd go have a quick snack with the Balzac crowd and then I'd go meet my friend Lenore and we'd order some fresh bunting for the Alexandria Library Fire Memorial. At last year's Lament the purple seemed frayed and there were one or two comments. But I never got to do any of these things because I had a strange feeling that stopped me in my tracks. I'd heard enough about it previously to know what it was."

"Written?" Marina asked a third passionate time. "What was it like?"

"Don't go by me, Cookie," Pearl counselled. "It wasn't much for me. But Rosalind used to say that it was just like hearing your name called in that accidental key so that for a moment you really know it's your name."

"Then what happened?" Marina asked without looking to see where she was putting her cup.

"I thought I was going to be sick. The world commenced to wobble and my clothes went gray. My head began to fill with rural metaphors. I found myself in a big kitchen surrounded by busy people with trays. I was expected to carve silly, pinwheely things out of fruit. I tried to look like I knew what I was doing but when I opened my mouth to ask for more oranges I discovered that I had an accent. I needed air."

Pearl paused a second to indulge herself in a full shudder over the recollected terror of her brief protagonism.

"I pushed open the kitchen doors and looked out on the grand dining room. It was a revolting sight; a vast swarm of grabbers and wasters and gluttons. I felt like I'd been betrothed to a monstrosity. But I promised myself I'd stick it out. Kitchen work is honest work, I told myself.

"But they went too damn far when they sent me that rich boy to marry. Out of the question. Innocent women might read my book and hope for rich boys. The chance of a rich boy might keep them quiet. 'I won't be in this dream,' I swore."

"But what could you do?" Marina asked.

"The next time I had that funny feeling, I gritted everything and made myself concentrate on nonsense; limericks, jabberwocky, anything.

"And it worked, too. First, the editor called the author. Said he'd been giving the manuscript a quick reread and it struck him that the character of Pearl didn't quite come through. He said that the publisher agreed with him.

"The author took us all home and tried to fix me. He tried every trick he knew. Changed my hair, gave me a limp. But nothing worked. I wouldn't come. I was gone for good and I'd left a large hole behind me. He turned his powers of imagination to thinking up a good explanation to tell his friends.

"But what did the other characters in the book do?" Marina asked. "Did they know that it was because of you?"

"They knew and they were furious. There was a quick show trial. My defense was easily stated. 'I can't be in this dream,' I told them. 'I want to make a new world and shake things up. It's my job.'

"But it was too threatening. Everything, the economy, their way of life, everything depended on stopping me. I never really expected it to go any other way."

"But why come here?" Marina asked. "I mean of all places. Isn't Doeville the capital of what you hate?"

"You bet." Pearl stretched. "That's what makes it the most natural place to struggle. I'm trying to organize the stereotypes. It's slow, frustrating work, believe me. But someday they'll rise up and break the dead relationships and in their liberation we'll find new stories."

Marina and Pearl embraced each other. They were friends like soldiers. It was what Marina had always wanted.

"Should I stay in Doeville with you?" Marina was afraid that she knew what the answer would be. "I will if you want me to."

"No, go back to my friends and get written." Pearl felt one of her soul's long unused tendons unflexing. She wondered when the ache would pass and how much she would miss it. "Just don't end up in a book entitled Whither anything and you'll be alright. If you're lucky, you'll be dangerous. We'll be in touch."

They slept until it was almost dark the following rainy day. They ate french toast for dinner, Marina praying all the time that there would be a disaster to keep the Zephyr from running. Pearl insisted that Marina take her heather sweater. They stood by the doorway.

"I can't go. I want to stay here with you. I never felt real until I came here," Marina confided.

"Real? Don't you know, Marina," Pearl said plaintively. She opened the front door. The blue sky was cut by big rouge fingers hanging high over the neat houses. "For most people, reality *is* heaven. They just can't get it."

XIII

ALL THE WAY TO HEAVEN IS HEAVEN

IF IT WEREN'T FOR THE Beethoven, Marina wouldn't have known that anyone was there. Roger's house was dark. He sat cross-legged on the living room floor, moving fervently in the shocking directions of the Grosse Fugue.

The music was conducting him. His face contorted in anguished communion with a raving cello. It was abruptly released into rapture by the veer of a delirious violin. He made no sign that he was aware of her presence and Marina speculated that it might have something to do with her trip to Pearl. At the end of the fugue she carefully lifted the needle off the record.

"Roger, it's me," she said softly. "I'm home."

"Marina! How long have you been here?" Roger slapped himself. "I'm sorry; it's the music. I get lost in it."

"Oh, that's okay," she reassured him, relieved to know he wasn't angry. "I liked watching you."

"Sit down! Sit down!" he pleaded, jumping to his feet. "I have so much to tell you. Something miraculous happened to me. Something staggering."

"Me first," she teased.

"No, no, no. It's too amazing! I promise."

"More amazing than what I have to tell you about Pearl? And me?" Marina was certain that Roger was going to tell her about some minor triumph at the baseball game.

"Alright. Alright." He felt he could afford to be magnanimous. "Tonight we'll be saving the best for last. You go right ahead."

Marina hadn't stopped to think until just that moment that her news might be a terrible blow to Roger's hopes.

"I'm a fool, Roger."

"That's your news? I hardly know what to say. It's not exactly stop the presses."

Marina was disarmed. "No," she laughed. "Maybe it'll be alright. Roger, I won't be able to help you. I've discovered that I'm just another character. I'm just like you.

"Oh, but this is wonderful! I should've known." He surprised her with the power of his embrace. "It makes perfect sense to me. You came to us in our time of need. Stay here with me and we'll be friends and maybe more if there is more. My emptiness is finished. Why, think of it, we might even end up in the same book together!"

"I'd like that. I feel good in this house. Peaceful. Even that first night, which seems like years ago."

"Yes, lots of time, squeezed into a couple of days. More life than in all my centuries. And Pearl?" he asked lightly.

"Still Pearl, you'll be glad to know. I never met anyone like her. I don't even know how to talk about her.

Except that she sends you her deep love and she's more awake and valiant than ever before. I told her to expect you in the near future."

"And the sky?" Roger asked. "Have you managed to fix that, too?"

"No. The sky depends on all of us. The world has lost too many worlds already. We have their broken pitchers and tiny shreds of their clothing, but we can't hear their voices. They're quiet forever." Marina took a deep breath. "I have some ideas and I trust people.

"Now tell me your big news."

"No." It was a jubilant refusal.

"Roger, if you're really serious about us living together, you're going to have to stop being so . . ." She paused to search for a word that wouldn't offend. ". . . so tricky."

"I'm not tricky. I'll tell this story the best way I know how. That means putting old Opus 130 on the turntable and opening a bottle of champagne. I estimate this will take a big two minutes. I'll meet you on the living room floor."

"Such precision," she mused affectionately as she sank down on her knees. She was gratified to know him well. "All this preparation, stagecraft, just for a little baseball story."

Roger returned shortly, juggling a swaddled bottle of champagne, glasses and a pewter candlestick.

"Is it alright if I turn on the light?" she asked rhetorically, reaching up to the lamp.

"No. I want you to hear this in the dark because I want you to really hear it. Maybe you should even close your eyes. It's up to you."

Marina took a long look at Roger. "He's made some kind of serious trade," she thought. "The dizziness is gone."

"Something really did happen to you today," she said softly.

"Yes, Marina."

She closed her eyes.

"Thank you," he said.

When he was satisfied that everything was the way it should be, he turned on the record player. Marina was patiently dreamy as he lilted in militant ecstasy to the whole first movement.

"I have this feeling," he said loosening his tie, "that the world is ready to be." He re-entered the second movement for the length of a phrase.

"I'd like to tell you what happened to me today." He took a tight sip of champagne. "Well, naturally I didn't make the team again this year." He fended off the first syllable of a commiseration and shook his head. "It doesn't hurt anymore. Besides, the way the light was, the colors of the uniforms against the green field, the caps that fly off and sail back to the ground when things get fast —just to see it was to be part of it. I wasn't sad at all." They kissed.

"As I was saying, the field was a marvelous vision this day. Raskolnikov had a no-hitter going into the seventh and with that all-Karamazov outfield behind him, stopping everything like a net, he was not a noticeably worried man. Even Vronsky, who never liked catching lefties, and especially this particular lefty, had to admit that Raskolnikov seemed to have the situation well in hand. The score was three-zip.

"Two more hitless, breathless innings and the Rusky Rascal isn't even tired. With one out left, Ahab decides to send in Tom Jones to pinch hit. Jones has been begging for a crack at it and Ahab figures that the game is already over.

"Raskolnikov's first pitch is a little wild and Tom takes this as a good sign. His next pitch is more controlled, but still low and away. Then bang, bang; two smokey, murderous strikes. Jones' face squints flat. He's desperate to drive the next ball and his own impending past tense very far away.

"I'll see his face forever, frozen at the sight of another fast ball he knows he can't find. He swings at pure nothing, coming down hard on one knee and looking horrified away from the earth, as if to say, 'Oh God, you've left me for someone new.'

"It was something that had to be shared, so I turn to the man on my left. And it's unmistakably him, Marina. The broad, brainy forehead, the straggly hair; it's no one but Shakespeare, the man I've been looking for."

The home-starved strains of the cavatina of the quartet was plaiting itself into the night and the story. Marina moved closer to Roger.

"People are beginning to stand up and leave the park. I can't just let him vanish. He tries to get by me. Our eyes meet and I say, very nervously, passing my shaky hand across the horizon, The light, the field, the capacities of a lonely man. Isn't it too beautiful for words?'

"And Shakespeare, he says, 'Nothing is.'"

ANN DRUYAN is an author, lecturer, producer, and director who focuses on the effects of science and technology on our civilization. She was creative director of NASA's Voyager Interstellar Message Project. With her late husband, Carl Sagan, she wrote the original TV series *Cosmos: A Personal Voyage,* and she created two new seasons of Cosmos, for which she received Emmy, Peabody, and Producer Guild awards. Druyan and Sagan also cowrote six New York Times best-sellers, including *Shadows of Forgotten Ancestors,* and created the motion picture *Contact.* She has lectured at Harvard University, Cambridge University, CalTech, the Washington National Cathedral, and the Musée d'Art Moderne de Paris.